Little Joe's Boat Race

by Andy Blackford

Illustrated by Tim Archbold

FRANKLIN WATTS
LONDON•SYDNEY

First published in 2010 by
Franklin Watts
338 Euston Road
London
NW1 3BH

Franklin Watts Australia
Level 17/207 Kent Street
Sydney
NSW 2000

A CIP catalogue record for this book is available from the British Library.

ISBN 978 0 7496 9457 9 (hbk)
ISBN 978 0 7496 9467 8 (pbk)

Series Editor: Jackie Hamley
Series Advisor: Catherine Glavina
Series Designer: Peter Scoulding

Printed in China

Franklin Watts is a divison of
Hachette Children's Books,
an Hachette UK company.
www.hachette.co.uk

It was the day of the Village Boat Race. Little Joe took his boat along.

The other boys laughed at him.

"Your boat's FAR too small, Little Joe! And so are YOU!"

Little Joe sat by the river
and watched the race.

The biggest boat started to drift towards the rocks.

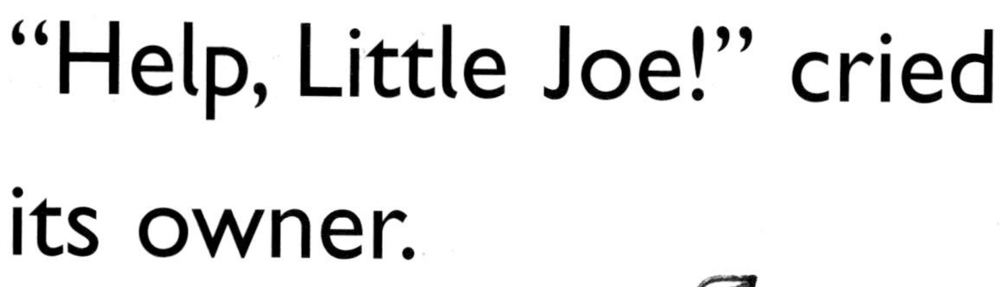

"Help, Little Joe!" cried its owner.

Only Joe was light enough to climb on the branch ...

... and reach the boat.

Then he fell! He landed on the boat as it raced towards the rapids!

Little Joe managed to steer the boat between the rocks.

A swan thought he was trying to steal her eggs.

She tried to peck him.

After a while, the river reached the sea.

The sky turned black.
First it began to rain.

Then it hailed.

Little Joe saw a huge whale

It was stuck on the rocks.

Little Joe raced to the rescue.

He threw a rope to the whale and pulled it off the rocks.

Then the wind dropped and the boat stopped moving.

But the whale pulled Little Joe and the boat back towards home.

A big crowd was waiting on the shore to cheer him.

The boys from the village were there, too.

"Well done, Little Joe!" they cried. "You're the best sailor in the whole village!"

Puzzle 1

Put these pictures in the correct order.
Now tell the story in your own words.
How short can you make the story?

Puzzle 2

helpful selfish
determined

worried nervous
happy

Choose the words which best describe the characters. Can you think of any more? Pretend to be one of the characters!

Answers

Puzzle 1

The correct order is:

1d, 2e, 3a, 4f, 5c, 6b

Puzzle 2

Little Joe The correct words are determined, helpful.

The incorrect word is selfish.

Boat owners The correct words are nervous, worried.

The incorrect word is happy.

Look out for more Leapfrog stories:

The Little Star
ISBN 978 0 7496 3833 7

Mary and the Fairy
ISBN 978 0 7496 9142 4

Jack's Party
ISBN 978 0 7496 4389 8

Pippa and Poppa
ISBN 978 0 7496 9140 0

The Bossy Cockerel
ISBN 978 0 7496 9141 7

The Best Snowman
ISBN 978 0 7496 9143 1

Big Bad Blob
ISBN 978 0 7496 7092 4*
ISBN 978 0 7496 7796 1

Cara's Breakfast
ISBN 978 0 7496 7797 8

Croc's Tooth
ISBN 978 0 7496 7799 2

The Magic Word
ISBN 978 0 7496 7800 5

Tim's Tent
ISBN 978 0 7496 7801 2

Why Not?
ISBN 978 0 7496 7798 5

Sticky Vickie
ISBN 978 0 7496 7986 6

Handyman Doug
ISBN 978 0 7496 7987 3

Billy and the Wizard
ISBN 978 0 7496 7985 9

Sam's Spots
ISBN 978 0 7496 7984 2

Bill's Baggy Trousers
ISBN 978 0 7496 3829 0

Bill's Bouncy Shoes
ISBN 978 0 7496 7990 3

Bill's Scary Backpack
ISBN 978 0 7496 9458 6*
ISBN 978 0 7496 9468 5

Little Joe's Big Race
ISBN 978 0 7496 3832 0

Little Joe's Balloon Race
ISBN 978 0 7496 7989 7

Little Joe's Boat Race
ISBN 978 0 7496 9457 9*
ISBN 978 0 7496 9467 8

Felix on the Move
ISBN 978 0 7496 4387 4

Felix and the Kitten
ISBN 978 0 7496 7988 0

Felix Takes the Blame
ISBN 978 0 7496 9456 2*
ISBN 978 0 7496 9466 1

The Cheeky Monkey
ISBN 978 0 7496 3830 6

Cheeky Monkey on Holiday
ISBN 978 0 7496 7991 0

Cheeky Monkey's Treasure Hunt
ISBN 978 0 7496 9455 5*
ISBN 978 0 7496 9465 4

*hardback